THE MEMORY CUPBOARD

A Thanksgiving Story

Charlotte Herman   Paintings by **Ben F. Stahl**

Albert Whitman & Company
Morton Grove, Illinois

Library of Congress Cataloging-in-Publication Data

Herman, Charlotte.
The memory cupboard : a Thanksgiving story / by Charlotte Herman; illustrated by Ben F. Stahl.
p. cm.
Summary: When Katie breaks a gravy boat at Thanksgiving dinner, her grandmother shows her that love is more important than objects.
ISBN 0-8075-5055-8 (hardcover)
[1. Grandmothers—Fiction. 2. Thanksgiving Day—Fiction. 3. Family—Fiction.] I. Stahl, Ben F., ill. II. Title.
PZ7.H4313Me 2003 [E]—dc21 2003000237

The paintings were done in acrylic on board.
The design is by Carol Gildar.

For more information about Albert Whitman & Company, please visit our web site at www.albertwhitman.com.

Thanks to my brother, Irv Baran, for taking the chocolate out of the cupboard.—C.H.

With love to my granddaughters:
Leah Nechama, Leah Chaya, Ariella, and Shoshana,
and to my Yonatan.—C.H.

To my wife, Pat—B.F.S.

It was Thanksgiving, and Mom, Dad, and I were visiting my grandma, who lived far away. "East of the Mississippi," Dad told me. It took us two nights and a day to get there by train.

Mom's brother, Uncle Eddie, met us at the station.

"There's my little Katie!" he said when he saw me. And he picked me up and twirled me around. "How's my most beautiful and favorite niece?"

"I'm your *only* niece," I said, laughing. "And I'm getting dizzy."

"Come on," said Uncle Eddie. "Everyone's waiting to see you."

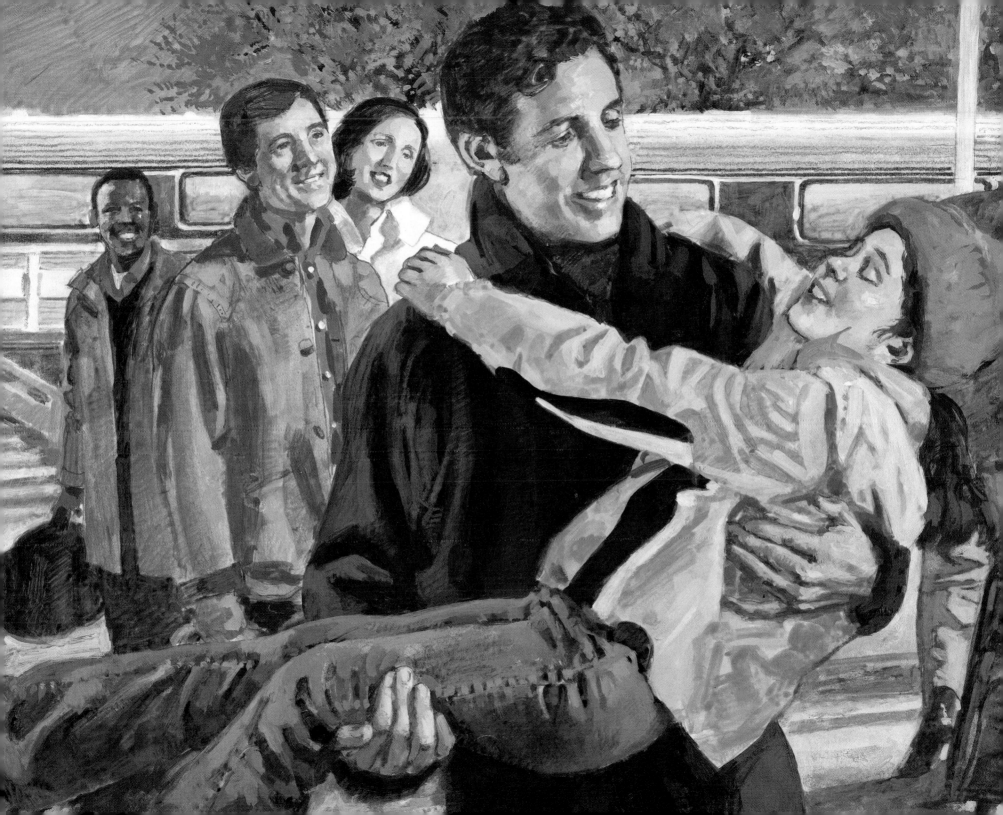

We drove through lightly falling snow to Grandma's big white house, the house where Mom and Uncle Eddie grew up.

"Better watch out," Uncle Eddie warned as we got out of the car. "You're gonna be bombarded!"

And sure enough, the family came swooping down on us with smiles and hugs. There was Great-Uncle Bernie, Great-Aunts Barbara and Laura, and Aunt Ruth, with little Davy asleep in her arms.

Then, finally, there was Grandma, smelling of spices and cinnamon. She held my face between her hands and said, "Such a sweet face, just like your mom's." And she kissed me on the forehead.

The relatives sat around talking, and when Grandma left for the kitchen, I followed her.

Right away I noticed the letters and drawings I'd sent her during the year. "You keep everything," I said.

"This is how I keep track of how you're growing," Grandma said. "This is how we stay close between phone calls and visits."

Grandma placed the turkey on a platter. "It's time, Katie," she said. And I knew what I was supposed to do. I plucked a small glass bell from a shelf and walked around the living room, ringing the bell and calling, "Turkey time! Turkey time!"

My call brought everyone into the dining room.

Grandma came in with the turkey, and Mom brought stuffing and sweet potatoes.

"This is a feast fit for a king," said Great-Uncle Bernie.

"The turkey looks too pretty to carve," said Great-Aunt Barbara.

"I've been waiting for Thanksgiving all year!" said Aunt Ruth.

And we all sat down at the table.

Uncle Eddie carved the turkey. "Say, where's our old turkey platter? The one with the little turkeys running along the border? I've never seen this one before."

"Oh, I decided it was time for a change," said Grandma with a wave of her hand. "Let's eat."

I took some of everything because I was so hungry. Grandma served the gravy in a white gravy boat. I traced the blue flowers with my finger.

"Your mom and Uncle Eddie bought me this for Mother's Day a long time ago," Grandma said when she saw me admiring the gravy boat.

"We saw it in a store window," Mom said. "And we knew that Grandma just had to have it."

"We broke into both of our piggy banks," Uncle Eddie continued. "But we didn't have enough money. So your grandpa gave us the rest."

We had a wonderful time, eating and singing. Great-Aunt Laura led us in her favorite song, "Over the River and Through the Woods." And then it was time to clear the table for dessert.

I wanted to help. I picked up the gravy boat carefully in both hands. But the next thing I knew, it had slipped out of my hands and crashed to the floor.

There was complete silence. When I looked down at the floor and saw that beautiful gravy boat broken in pieces, I burst into tears.

Grandma looked at the pieces and then at me. Without a word, she took my hand and led me away. Where were we going?

I was still crying as she led me out of the kitchen and up the back stairway into the little guest room. It had a bed, a rocking chair, and a tall wooden cupboard painted white.

Grandma took a brass key from a hook on the window frame and inserted it into the cupboard's keyhole. She opened the door and announced, "Behold! My memory cupboard. This is where I store my memories."

I saw shelves of toys, teapots, mugs, cookie jars, clocks, dolls, and porcelain ladies. So many things.

When I looked more closely, I saw that everything was broken! Humpty Dumpty was sitting at the base of a lamp. For an egg he was not in very good shape. Just like in the nursery rhyme, he was cracked.

"I don't understand," I said to Grandma. "I don't see any memories. All I see are broken things."

"Ah, but what *I* see are memories. Every object here has a story to tell."

Grandma reached into the cupboard and brought out a
striped mug with a chipped rim. "Grandpa's favorite coffee mug,
for instance. Whenever I look at it, I see Grandpa at the table
enjoying his morning coffee."

"How did it get chipped?" I asked.

"From years of use. Loving use," said Grandma. She sniffed
the mug. "You know, I do believe I can still smell the coffee."

I sniffed, too, but I couldn't smell anything.

"Tell me about Humpty Dumpty," I said.

Grandma wiped a speck of dust from Humpty's cracked head. "Grandpa and I told your mom and Uncle Eddie years of bedtime stories by the light of this lamp. One day they were chasing each other around the room. And Humpty Dumpty had a great fall."

I laughed, and so did Grandma.

"And now I'll tell you a little secret," said Grandma.

"Just today, as I was washing this . . ."
She reached into the cupboard and took out
the old turkey platter, the one with the little
turkeys running around the border. A chunk
of the platter was missing.

"I knocked the platter against the faucet,"
she explained. "I'm afraid I killed a turkey or
two."

"Oh, I'm sorry," I said.

"It's OK," said Grandma, returning the
platter to the cupboard. "It doesn't matter."

She sat down on the bed, patted a place
for me next to her, and put her arm around me.

"And it doesn't matter about the gravy
boat, either. Sometimes, no matter how
careful we are, things we're fond of get broken.
But things are just things. People are more
important, especially granddaughters."

Grandma smiled at me. "We can glue the gravy boat together," she said. "And whenever I look at it, I'll still see your mom and Uncle Eddie, so proud and excited the day they gave it to me. And I'll remember today, when I shared my memory cupboard with you."

I knew I would remember, too.

We heard Mom calling from downstairs.

"Let's go," said Grandma. "We have lots more Thanksgiving memories to make."